THE DELUXE
MOVIE NOVELIZATION

Adapted by Stacia Deutsch

Simon Spotlight

New York   London   Toronto   Sydney   New Delhi

VISTA GRANDE
PUBLIC LIBRARY

SIMON SPOTLIGHT
An imprint of Simon & Schuster Children's Publishing Division
1230 Avenue of the Americas, New York, New York 10020
First Simon Spotlight hardcover edition June 2018
TM & © 2018 Sony Pictures Animation Inc. All Rights Reserved.
Also available in a Simon Spotlight paperback edition titled *Hotel Transylvania 3 Movie Novelization*.
All rights reserved, including the right of reproduction in whole or in part in any form.
SIMON SPOTLIGHT and colophon are registered trademarks of Simon & Schuster, Inc. For information about special discounts for bulk purchases, please contact Simon & Schuster Special Sales at 1-866-506-1949 or business@simonandschuster.com.
Book designed by Nick Sciacca
The text of this book was set in Caslon Antique.
Manufactured in the United States of America 0418 LAK
10 9 8 7 6 5 4 3 2 1
ISBN 978-1-5344-2152-3 [hc]
ISBN 978-1-5344-1331-3 [*Hotel Transylvania 3 Movie Novelization* pbk]
ISBN 978-1-5344-1332-0 [*Hotel Transylvania 3 Movie Novelization* eBook]

HOTEL TRANSYLVANIA 3

SUMMER VACATION

CHAPTER ONE

In 1897

The Transylvania Express barreled down the train tracks at top speed. Passengers dressed up for the journey. Riding a fine train like this one was a privilege. It was a beautiful day for travel.

The conductor walked down the aisle calling out the next stop. "Budapest . . . Budapest . . . Ze next stop, Budapest." He stopped as he approached five very strange-looking old ladies. They were all dressed in oversized overcoats and had their heads covered . . . so that the only skin that showed was their hands.

The train conductor was used to odd-looking passengers. "Tickets, ladies?" he asked casually.

The women all handed over their tickets to get punched by the conductor.

"Here you go!" a high-pitched voice said. It was coming from a giant woman whose hand was blue and covered with stitches.

"Here's mine," said the next woman, whose hand was pale and had long nails.

"...and mine!" said another, whose hand was covered in fur.

"Mine too," said the next, whose hand was stubby and covered in bandages.

"Here you go," said the last one, whose ticket came from a gloved hand ... but the wrist was invisible. The conductor either didn't notice, or didn't care.

"Eh ... thank you, young ... man!" said the woman with the pale skin and long nails.

The conductor didn't realize these weren't women at all. In fact, they weren't human. This was a group of Transylvania's finest monsters, known far and wide as the Drac Pack: Dracula plus his friends Frank, Griffin,

Murray, and Wayne. They were all disguised as Eastern European old ladies.

The conductor went back to punching tickets, and the monsters felt they could relax a little.

"Man, I hate wearing disguises. These heels are killing me," Murray said. His feet were crammed into tiny shoes.

"I love it! I never get to dress up," Griffin exclaimed. Since Griffin was invisible, he usually just wore glasses so his friends would know he was there.

"Take it down a notch, fellas," Dracula warned. "We don't want to alarm the humans."

Too late. Frank had just noticed that a little boy was staring at them . . . and starting to whimper.

"*Pssst.* Drac?" Frank whispered, but then the boy began to cry.

"I'm about to *undt* freak out!" the boy said, in a German accent.

Drac acted quickly to hypnotize the boy to make him think he was a cat. "You're a nice kitty," he said, and the boy began to meow like a cat.

"I'm *undt* kitty cat. Meow, meow, meow," the boy

said, and licked his hand as if it was a paw.

Suddenly the doors in the back of the train burst open. Abraham Van Helsing, carrying an impressively large device, stepped in.

The passengers gasped!

Dracula sighed. "Oh no, not this clown again."

"Good evening, travelers! I am Professor Abraham Van Helsing. Yes! One of *the* Van Helsings! For centuries my family has battled monsters, so you can believe me when I tell you—there are monsters hiding amongst you!" His beady eyes scanned the faces of the passengers. "But fear not, for I am a professional and I know how to flush out these beasts and bring them into the light! Ahahahahaha." Van Helsing cackled and took out a box of matches from his jacket. He lit a match and held it under Frank's nose.

Frank tried desperately to stay calm but couldn't stand it. He jumped up and ripped off his disguise.

"FIRE BAD!!! Raaahhh!" Frank roared.

"The jig is up!" Drac said to his friends. "Go!"

All the monsters started to flee, just as a man with a cart offering root beer floats and pies came down the aisle.

"Root beer floats. Floats and pies . . . ," he said, oblivious to what was happening until he was almost trampled by the gang. Pies and floats went flying.

In a fit of fury, Van Helsing tried to blast the monsters.

The Drac Pack climbed onto the top of the train and ran. . . . Van Helsing climbed up too, and they just barely dodged the blasts. As they jumped from one train car to the next, Van Helsing followed.

When they got to the end of the train, Drac looked at his friends and then back at Van Helsing.

"Sorry, guys," he apologized as he pushed them off the train car to safety.

Van Helsing cornered Dracula at the end of the last train car.

"Finally! First I kill Dracula, and then the rest of the monsters!" the hunter growled in victory.

Dracula was calm. "Why do you keep doing this? Your dad, your grandfather, and your great-great-granny . . . I defeated them all. When will you Van Helsings ever learn to let go of the hate?"

"Never! Because you, monster, are a—"

He didn't finish, because Dracula transformed into a mouse.

"Eh, Squeak, Squeak," Drac said.

Van Helsing was confused. "Wha—? A mouse?"

Just then, the train went into a tunnel and Van Helsing, still standing tall, smashed into the bricks.

SPLAT.

"Ahhh." Van Helsing held his aching head.

This was just the beginning of Van Helsing's chase. The instant his head stopped swimming, the monster hunter got off the train and climbed into a biplane. He chased a bat as it swooped through the air. It was Drac!

"You can't run from me, Prince of Darkness. I will hunt you for all eternity—" Van Helsing shouted when Drac dove to the right and Van Helsing's plane kept going straight, slamming into the side of a mountain. "AAHHOOW!"

Next, Drac turned into a wolf and ran through the street. This time, Van Helsing chased him in a 1920s-style car.

"I swear I will never rest until I destroy you—" Van

Helsing said, but he didn't get a chance to finish his sentence.

Dracula disappeared in front of a brick wall, and Van Helsing's car crashed with a SPLAT!

"OOF!" Van Helsing whimpered.

Van Helsing refused to give up the chase.

This time, the vampire simply appeared as himself, standing on the edge of a cliff.

"And—" Van Helsing said, trying to tell Drac his message as he stalked closer and closer.

The cliff crumbled, Dracula levitated in midair, and Van Helsing fell.

SPLAT!

In a cave, Dracula was in bat form.

Van Helsing had his blaster pointed directly at the vampire's head.

"Every—" Van Helsing began to say the rest of the message, but he was cut short again. A stalactite fell from the ceiling of the cave. "Oooh," he said as he watched it drop straight toward him.

SPLAT!

The next time Van Helsing cornered Drac, all he

could say was "Other—" before a giant metal gate came crashing onto him.

Van Helsing tried again. "Monster—" he blurted out, seconds before a giant spiky wrecking ball slammed into his face!

Van Helsing tried standing in front of another wall.

"If-it's-the-last-thing—" he yelled out, as quickly as possible. Then a wooden cart slammed him into the wall.

"I—" he tried, before a large battering ram crashed into his face.

"Ever—" he said, as a rock smacked his head.

"Dooooooooooo!" Van Helsing yelled as he fell from the top of a large cliff.

Dracula watched as Van Helsing landed in the ocean. When he bubbled to the surface, spitting and gasping for air, Dracula asked, "The last thing you ever *what*? Sorry, I didn't hear that last part...."

CHAPTER TWO

Present Day

All of that—from the need for disguises to being chased by Van Helsing—seemed like ancient history now that Drac had built Hotel Transylvania. It was a hotel where monsters could be safe from the outside world, and from people like Van Helsing.

Tonight, there was a wedding at the hotel. Zombie Beethoven, Zombie Mozart, and Zombie Bach had been playing lovely music for guests in the courtyard, waiting for the bride to walk down the aisle.

Drac noticed that the groom, a spiky monster named Carl, was sweating. Drac followed Carl's eyes down the aisle to where the bride should have been. Then Drac began sweating too.

The Drac Pack were among the guests, and Wayne had brought his wolf pups. He was carrying them in multiple baby carriers, and they were starting to get fussy. "Shh, shh," he hushed them. "When is this thing starting?" he asked. At that, the wolf pups started to cry.

"Aw, you made them cry, Wayne," Frank teased. "Oh, except this little one. Coochie, coochie, coochie," he said, smiling at the smallest and cutest of the bunch.

"That's Sunny," Wayne said. "She doesn't cry . . ."

Frank leaned in and tickled Sunny's chin. She bit his finger!

". . . she bites," Wayne added, a little late.

Up at the altar where the wedding ceremony was about to begin, Drac spoke to the groom.

"This is a very special moment, Carl," Drac said. "Any second your beautiful bride is going to walk right down the aisle."

They stared at the doors. The doors didn't open.

Carl gulped. "Oh no, Drac, she's not coming," he replied, still sweating from nerves.

Drac was calm. "Don't worry. Mavis is with her, and I'm sure she has everything under control." Drac turned and discreetly spoke into his headset, whispering, "Mavey, is everything under control?"

Upstairs, in the bridal suite, Mavis was the wedding coordinator. She also had a headset.

"Uhmmmmm . . . yep. Just a slight case of pre-wedding jitters," she told her dad.

Lucy was a spiky monster, like Carl, and she was shaking so hard, spikes shot out of her as she cried. One spike cut right through Eunice's hair, pulling it off . . . and revealing that Eunice was wearing a wig. Eunice snagged the wig and tried to put it back on quickly.

Another spike punctured a can of hair spray that then flew around the room, and another went through the rope that held up the chandelier, sending it crashing to the ground.

Drac heard all of this commotion over his headset.

"Yep! Everything is fine here . . . ," Mavis lied to her dad. She turned her attention to the bride. "Please try to relax, Lucy. I've taken care of everything. The wedding is going to be perfect."

"It's not that. It's just . . . how do I know I'm doing the right thing?" Lucy cried. As she blew her nose into a handkerchief, another spike shot out of her.

"I know just how you feel," Mavis said. "The day I married Johnny was the best day of my life, but I was so nervous . . ." Mavis started her story.

Drac was still listening on the headset and spoke up. "Not as nervous as I was."

Mavis blocked out his voice and went on. "And you should've seen my dad. He was a mess!"

"I wouldn't get outta my coffin that night," Drac agreed.

"But he knew it was meant to be. It doesn't matter where you come from, or how different you are—a zing only happens once in your life, and you have to cherish it."

Lucy smiled, and her eyes suddenly filled with happy tears. All of the bridesmaids sighed.

Downstairs at the ceremony site, Dracula sighed too.

"So it's very simple. When you first met Carl, did you zing?" Mavis asked.

Lucy thought about it, before saying, "Yes."

"Then what are you waiting for?" Mavis asked her.

"You're right! Thank you!" Lucy jumped up and hugged Mavis.

"Ha-ha, okay, all right," Mavis soothed Lucy, while trying to move out of the way as more spikes flew.

A few minutes later, Lucy and Carl were standing at the altar. Blobby greeted the bride and groom. He was leading the ceremony and asked them the important question.

"Blublubububuh?" Blobby asked Carl.

"I do," Carl said, looking tenderly at Lucy.

"Blububububububuh?" Blobby asked Lucy.

"I do," said Lucy.

As they kissed, Mavis and Drac heard a rumbling noise coming from the hotel and locked eyes.

"Do you hear that?" Mavis asked Drac.

"I thought we locked him in his room," Drac replied.

"We did!" Mavis insisted.

At that moment, Tinkles, a giant dog, ran through the wedding party with Dennis and Winnie riding on his back. Dennis was Mavis and Johnny's son, and Winnie was Wayne and Wanda Werewolf's oldest daughter.

"Hi, Mom! Hi, Papa!" Dennis said, as if nothing out of the ordinary was going on.

"Dennis!" Mavis and Drac yelled at once.

Dennis tried to explain. "Tinkles was crying, so we let him out!"

At that, Tinkles barked.

Drac tried to get control. "Tinkles, sit!" he ordered. Tinkles stopped, and Dennis and Winnie slid off his back while Drac clipped a leash onto Tinkles. "Come on, Tinkles. A wedding is no place for a doggie."

"Poor Tinkles," Winnie said.

Drac sighed. "Ugh. Who's idea was it to let Dennis have a puppy?" he asked over the headset.

"Yours!" Mavis replied.

Drac knew she was right. After all, he was the papa, and the kind of grandparent who wanted to give his grandkid everything he wanted.

Later, at the wedding reception, Johnny was the DJ and everyone was dancing.

"DJ Jazzy Johnny in the house! It's time to welcome the happy couple, Mr. and Mrs. Prickles!" Johnny announced.

Lucy and Carl entered to applause, and Johnny played a slow song. Carl and Lucy took the floor for the bride and groom dance.

"The bride and groom invite everyone to join them on the dance floor," Johnny said.

The monster couples all joined in. Wayne grabbed Wanda to try to dance—even though they were both carrying wolf pups in baby carriers—but every time they got close, the wolf pups began fighting. So instead of dancing, they just held hands from a distance.

Meanwhile, Drac looked at all the couples dancing, and sighed, sad that he had no one to dance with.

Just then, a graceful hand tapped him on the shoulder and a smooth voice asked, "Care to dance?"

Drac turned to find a beautiful Frankenstein woman standing there in an elegant dress.

Frank, Murray, and Griffin, the Invisible Man, were hiding behind Bigfoot's giant ankle, watching to see what Drac would do.

"Yes, good evening," Drac said, not realizing that his friends were up to something.

"Is that her?" Wayne whispered to the others.

"Oooo! Watch out, now! She got stitches in all the right places," Murray said, staring.

Griffin looked at the woman and then at Frank. "Okay, there's no way *that* is related to you, Frank," Griffin said. They seemed to have so little in common.

"Well, she's my right arm's cousin," Frank replied.

They watched as Drac held out his hand politely and the woman took it with a huge, strong, *manly* arm, and then dipped Drac backward.

"Hehehe . . . oh!" Drac said, surprised.

"Ah! I see it now," Griffin said, looking from Frank's arm to the woman's and noticing a similarity.

It was clear that Dracula was uncomfortable.

"Uh . . . heh . . . Are you here for the bride or the groom?" Dracula asked.

The woman gave Dracula a long, hard look, then smiled. "I'm here for *you*."

Dracula didn't understand. "Excuse me?"

"Frank sent me. We're arm cousins twice removed." The woman stroked Drac's face with her stitched-up hand, twirled him, and then dipped him.

Drac's eyes widened. "Of course. Eh, I'd recognize that bicep anywhere."

"Didn't he tell you? He thought since we're both single, we might hit it off. Maybe go on a date," the woman suggested.

Drac got very nervous. "A date!" He laughed awkwardly. Then he used his powers to zap Johnny's DJ booth and change the music to something fast-paced to get him out of the romantic moment.

It worked.

"I love this song!" Frank's cousin Ginger said. "Don't you, Dracula? Oh. Where'd he go?" she added when she realized Drac was gone. She ran off to look for him.

Meanwhile, Drac was hiding by the big foot.

"What's the matter, Drac? You didn't like her?" Frank asked Drac.

"No offense, but you can't be too picky. You haven't had a date in a hundred years," Griffin said.

"Hate the game, not the player," Murray quoted. "Or, or wait, is it hate the player . . ."

"I'm sure she's very nice, but I didn't zing. . . ." Drac frowned.

Wayne said, "Who cares? Just start with a date, and before you know it there's a wedding, and then kids, and then kids, and then kids, and then kids, and then—" He snapped out of it. "Don't do it, Drac! Don't do it!"

The pups all started crying at once. The werewolf jiggled to rock them, trying to get them all back to sleep.

"Aww, you made them cry, Wayne." Dracula looked at the little werewolves. "Except this one." He smiled at the smallest and the most adorable one.

"That's Sunny," Murray said. "She doesn't cry . . ."

Drac leaned in and tickled her chin. She bit his finger!

"OOOW!" Dracula pried her off.

". . . she bites," Murray warned him too late.

Drac held his finger and laughed uncomfortably. "Look, guys, I appreciate your concern. But it's not up to me. You only zing once. Martha was my one true zing, and she's gone."

"I don't think Martha would have wanted you to be alone this long," Frank told him.

"Yeah, we're worried about you," Murray put in.

"Times have changed, buddy. You can even find

someone to zing with on your phone now," Griffin said.

"What? Really?" Dracula pulled out his phone, looked at it, then put it away. "No, no. I'm far too busy. I have Mavis and Dennis and the hotel and blah, blah, blah."

"Um, did you guys hear that?" Frank asked. "He actually said, 'blah, blah, blah'!"

"I don't say, 'blah, blah, blah,'" Drac insisted, but no one believed it.

CHAPTER THREE

Later, when he was alone inside the hotel attic, Dracula pushed a button on his cell phone, and the phone beeped.

"What can I help you with, Lord of Darkness?" the phone voice asked.

"Eh, uh, I'm looking for a zing." It was so awkward for Dracula to ask.

The phone beeped and then answered, "Okay, changing phone ring."

The phone rang, and Drac pushed the center button again.

"No, no, I'm looking for a *date*," Dracula tried to explain to the voice.

The phone beeped again and then answered, "The date is Friday, July thirteenth."

"No, no, no, no. I want to meet someone."

The phone beeped again, not getting it. "Understood. You want to eat dim sum."

"Are you kidding me right now? Don't you get it? I want to go on a date. I'm lonely," Dracula desperately tried to explain.

The phone beeped. "I understand," it said in a softer tone. "You want baloney."

Dracula groaned, frustrated.

In the upstairs hallway, Mavis walked toward her suite, clicking away on a large tablet. When she heard a noise coming from behind the attic door, she stopped to listen.

Drac was still frustrated, but now he was trying to use ZINGR, a monsters-only dating app on his phone.

He paced and groaned as he looked at a series of hideous female monsters and swiped left to say that he wasn't interested in dating them.

"Ugh, no. Ugh. Too many eyes. Too few eyes. Not into tentacles. Whoa, look at that hair. No ... I can't ..." He tried to dismiss them, but couldn't figure out how to swipe correctly with his long fingernail. He selected one of them by accident.

"Match Found!" the phone announced.

The app rang. It was connecting the call between him and the mystery monster.

A picture of a busty witch was on his screen with the screen name: Wicked_1. The video chat symbol appeared alongside the word "Connecting ..."

"No, no, no, no, no!" Dracula shrieked.

A witch's face emerged on his phone's screen. She looked even worse than in her picture, and was surrounded by cats.

She got straight to the point. "First things first," she told Drac before he could even say hello. "I'm not into games, you better have a job, and my cats have to like you." The many, many, cats all around her started meowing and hissing.

"Wooah!" Drac freaked out.

Just then, there was a knock on the door and Mavis

22

stuck her head into the attic. "Dad?" she asked, noticing his cell phone.

"Ohhh! Mavis!" Drac whirled around, shoving the phone into his pocket. "What are you doing here?"

"I was just checking on the honeymoon suite, and I heard something," Mavis said, looking at him suspiciously.

"Oh, uh . . . I'm sorry, my little bedbug. I, uh, I was cleaning the attic!" Drac whipped out a feather duster and started dusting, zipping around the attic. He hummed to himself, "Ahh da de de de, da doo di doo. Oh, so dirty!" He didn't know that the witch was still on the phone.

"Who is that?!" the witch asked, her voice muffled since the phone was still in Drac's pocket.

Mavis was confused about where the voice was coming from. "Are you on the phone?" she asked Drac.

"What? This?" Drac pulled the phone out of his pocket. "I was just trying to find a maid to help me with the mess."

The witch's voice called out, "A maid? Who do you think—"

Quickly Dracula spoke into the phone. "Thank you. I'll check your references and get back to you, good-bye!" He pushed a button to hang up the call and started dusting and humming nervously. "Ah do do di do do, doo doo di doo."

Mavis saw right through it. "Stop trying to hide it from me," Mavis said to Drac.

"Hide who, I mean, *what*? Me?" Drac stiffened up, instantly nervous.

"Yesssss," Mavis said. "And I know what it is."

Dracula gulped.

"You're stressed out from working too hard," Mavis guessed.

Drac exhaled with relief. "Okay, you got me. It's a big hotel, lots to do. But what about you? You're pretty busy yourself."

Mavis agreed. "I know. It seems like now that we're working together more, we're seeing each other less."

"Oh, hehe, you're absolutely right," Dracula agreed. "I am working too much. You're working too much. We should really take a break, but until then, night, night!" He escorted her out and quickly shut the door behind her.

As Dracula began to take out his phone, Mavis peeked back in.

"And, Dad?"

"Oh! Uh . . . Yes, Mavis?" Dracula paused.

"I love you," Mavis said.

"I love you, too, sweetheart." Dracula leaned forward and kissed Mavis on the forehead. "Sweet nightmares!"

She closed the door and walked off. With a sigh of relief, he leaned against the attic door.

The witch, who was still on the phone, spoke up and said, "I'm still here!"

Mavis returned to her bedroom, where Dennis and Johnny were snuggled together sleeping on top of the giant dog, Tinkles. The TV was on, playing a kung fu movie. Faint swooping and chopping sounds filled the room.

"Aww." Her family looked really cute, and there was plenty of room on the monster dog, so she crawled on to snuggle with them.

Johnny gave a huge yawn and stirred. "Hey, ready for daaaaaaate night?"

"No, honey, it's okay. You rest," Mavis said to him. Then to herself, she muttered, "You know, dad was right, we do need a break." She considered that thought. "We need to all be together again, like a family. Like we used to." Snuggling in tighter, she decided to turn off the TV, but instead of clicking it off, she accidentally turned up the volume.

On-screen, a fish man was talking. "Are you over-worked and stressed out?" he announced, and seemed to be speaking directly to her.

"Urgh," she snorted, fiddling with the remote, but then she began to listen to what the man was saying.

"Do you need some family time? Are you a monster? Then you need a vacation! A monster vacation!"

The music from the commercial kicked in, giving Mavis a brilliant idea.

She sat up on the dog and smiled.

High in the sky, a jumbo 747 jet flew smoothly across the night sky. Those people on that plane were the lucky ones.

Behind that plane was another one. The Gremlin Air plane struggled across the same bit of sky. The junky old 1940s plane was bumping up and down while a few unnecessary parts fell off. Or maybe they were necessary?

There were two gremlin pilots flying the plane. When bird poop hit the windshield, one of the gremlins crawled out of the plane and tried to wipe the poop off, but instead smeared it all over the pilot's window. The pilot couldn't see, but still gave a thumbs-up.

Back in the cabin, there was chaos as the gremlin flight crew acted wildly, throwing bags in the aisles and breaking every rule of human flight attendants.

A gremlin flight attendant stood in the front of the plane. "Ladies and gentlemen, please direct your attention to the front of the cabin." She held up a seat belt prop to do a demonstration. "For your safety, please *unbuckle* your seat belts."

A Cyclops monster did as he was told and unbuckled his seat belt just before the plane suddenly hit some major turbulence. He went flying through the roof of the plane and landed outside on the tail.

"Ahhh! Oof," he said, hanging on tight.

The flight attendant went on with her speech. "In the unlikely event that we experience a sudden drop in cabin pressure, oxygen will be provided." At that, a gremlin dropped down from the ceiling above Dr. Jekyll, who was quietly sitting in his seat. The gremlin grabbed Jekyll's face and blew air into his mouth.

The flight attendant went up to another monster who was holding his bag on his lap. "Can I stow that for you, sir?"

"All right, thanks," the monster replied.

The gremlin took his bag and threw it out the plane window.

Another gremlin pushed the snack trolley. "Beverages! Beverages! Snacks! Snacks! Beverages!" A different gremlin was riding on top of the snack trolley, throwing food in every direction. "Beverages! Snacks! Beverages! Snacks! Beverages! Snacks!" The trolley sped through the aisle. They hit a monster's elbow, and it spun all the way around.

The Human Fly stepped into the aisle and was immediately run over by the cart.

"Beverages! Beverages! Snacks! Beverages! Snacks!"

"Ahhh!" a yeti shrieked when his foot was crushed by the cart's wheel.

The flight attendant asked Murray for his drink request. "Coffee?"

"Sure," Murray answered, and in response the flight attendant poured the hot coffee directly onto Murray's lap.

"AHHH! AHH! AAAAAH!" Murray shouted.

In the rows behind him, Drac, Mavis, Johnny, Dennis, Frank and Eunice, Wayne and Wanda and their pups, Griffin, Blobby, and all their friends ordered snacks from the cart.

Everyone was excited for the big trip except Drac, who was complaining. "Mavis, pleeeease ... you're torturing me," he whined to Mavis.

That's because he had no idea where they were going.

"This is a fun surprise," Mavis retorted.

"There are no fun surprises! Just tell me where we're going. Why are we on a plane? We can fly, you know."

Vlad, who was sitting behind them, chimed in.

"Back in my day people took trains. Now, that's classy."

Drac rejected the idea that trains were better. "Sure, Dad, forty hours in a closet-sized room with you and Uncle Bernie and his smelly cigars, arguing who was more attractive, Cleopatra or Nefertiti."

Resigned, Dracula said, "Mavis, this is such an amazing surprise, and I can't wait to spend time with the people I love most, but I beg of you . . . tell me where we're going!"

"Nope," Mavis told him. "I've taken care of everything, so you don't need to worry. You've been so stressed out lately. It's time for you to relax."

She pushed the button and leaned back his chair, put headphones in his ears, a neck pillow around his neck, and slipped a sleep mask over his eyes. Then, she took off his shoes and put on slippers. Drac peeked out from his eye mask as Mavis covered him in a blanket. Forcing him to relax, she took out some lotion and massaged it onto his face.

"Now, isn't that better?" Mavis asked, looking at all she'd done.

"Oh ho ho ye-he-hes. Soooooo relaxed." Dracula sat up in his chair with lotion dripping off his face. He looked and felt ridiculous.

Johnny was sitting in the next row with Dennis and Winnie.

Dennis leaned over and whispered to Winnie, "I'm gonna go check on you know who." Then he announced loudly, "I have to go to the bathroom," so their dads wouldn't guess at the truth.

At the same time that Dennis snuck off, Johnny noticed a gremlin on the outside of the plane! He turned to Winnie, asking, "Did you see that?"

Winnie was so nervous that Dennis had snuck off, she blurted, "DENNIS WENT TO THE BATHROOM!"

"Uhhh . . . okay . . ." That seemed normal to Johnny.

At the back of the plane, Dennis snuck into the baggage area where he'd stowed Tinkles.

"Psst, where are you?" Dennis called in the darkness.

Tinkles whimpered, and his huge eyes peeked out from a large pile of suitcases. Dennis climbed up the pile and petted Tinkles to calm him down.

"Don't worry, Tinkles. We're almost there," Dennis told his dog.

The captain's voice came over the intercom, giving the opposite instructions of a typical captain. "Okay, folks. You are free to walk about the cabin as we've started our descent."

Outside the plane, under one wing, a gremlin quickly smacked the engine with a hammer, forcing the plane to instantly nose-dive at an incredible speed.

Dennis ran back to his seat and gave Winnie a thumbs-up, to let her know that Tinkles was okay.

Meanwhile, the gremlin pilots warmed up some tea and had a little chat.

"So, any big plans for the weekend, Rob?" the captain asked the pilot.

"Oh, you know, the usual. Gotta take the kids to soccer," the pilot replied.

The plane continued to nose-dive, and the flight attendants continued to roll the cart down the aisle, calling, "Snacks? Beverages? Snacks?"

The plane lost more and more parts and fell until it crashed into the ocean with a big splash.

When the plane bubbled back to the surface, the gremlin flight attendant announced, "Ladies and gentlemen, we've arrived at our destination, the Bermuda Triangle."

"Ooooo!" Frank looked out the window at a giant triangle-shaped hole in the ocean filled with a giant tower of wrecked ships.

Eunice peered out past him and echoed, "Ooooo!"

The plane, which was now a skeleton, floated into the triangle and plunged down the side of a waterfall. It splashed as it approached a sand bank where a ton of aircraft wreckage was stacked.

All the monsters gushed. "Look at that!" and "Cool!" and "Wow, oooh."

Drac, Mavis, Frank, Eunice, and the others filed out of the plane, through the wreckage. They discovered that this first old ship was connected to a newer ship, then a submarine, then up through another airplane, and finally they went through the door of an aircraft carrier at the surface.

A door opened and there stood Stan, the half fish, half man crew leader. He greeted the monsters at the door.

"Welcome to the Bermuda Triangle," Stan said cheerily, "where you'll embark on a monster cruise of a lifetime!" He gestured to a giant cruise ship . . . and it was in that moment that Drac finally realized where they were going.

"A cruise?" Drac asked.

"Surprise!" Mavis said.

"But it's just like a hotel . . . on the water," Drac said, trying to not sound disappointed.

"I just figured you need a vacation from running everyone else's vacation," Mavis explained. "You've barely been out of that hotel since, well, since Mom died. I know you have a lot of memories there, but this is a chance to make new memories. With all of us. With Dennis."

Just then, Dennis and Johnny walked in.

"BOOOOOOOOOOOAT!" Johnny cheered.

"BOOOOOOOOOOAT!" Dennis echoed.

Drac smiled. "Who made you such an amazing daughter?" he asked Mavis.

"You!" Mavis hugged her dad.

"Heee, that's right. What a father I am!" Dracula said as Johnny and Dennis joined them.

"Come on, Denisovich," Dracula said, getting into the idea of spending more time with Dennis. "Let's get cruisin'!"

CHAPTER FOUR

It was boarding time. Three witches soared in on brooms, cackling and circling the massive cruise ship. It was extremely impressive.

The monsters gathered in the ballroom, where fish men waiters brought them appetizers.

The anchor was raised, the horn blew, and the ship began to pull back from the port, sailing through the ocean.

Wayne, Wanda, and hundreds of wolf pups walked up to a photo backdrop for a family picture. The pups were going nuts, and as soon as they heard the photographer say, "Okay, smile!" they all stopped and smiled. But the instant the flash went off, the pups went nuts again.

"Thank you." Fish man Stan escorted them away as the next guests stepped to the photo area. He greeted his new monster family. "Welcome aboard! How are you doing? Nice to see you."

The witches finished circling the ballroom and landed on deck, next to a set of pool chairs. Each one snapped her fingers as their witch outfits poofed into bathing suits. The witches settled into pool chairs, stashing their brooms next to them. The last witch's broom refused to stand to the side. It took the last chair, and with a bit of magic, kicked the witch off, knocking her onto the deck.

Dennis looked around to see if the coast was clear while Winnie guided in a giant furry monster dressed in a trench coat and hat. It was Tinkles in disguise.

"Dennis, come on," Winnie said.

They walked up to the fish man greeter.

"Oh yes, hello, welcome aboard," the fish man said, looking up and down at the strange monster in front of him, who was actually Tinkles.

Dennis nudged Tinkles and said, "This is Bob. Say 'hi,' Bob," he instructed.

"Hi, Bob," Tinkles said.

Dennis, Tinkles, and Winnie walked past, trying to not draw attention to themselves.

On the deck, the Invisible Man was exploring the ship with his invisible girlfriend, Crystal, and the rest of the gang.

"Oh my gosh, Griffin. I am, like, so excited. This is, like, the nicest hotel I have ever been to."

Griffin shrugged. "Check it out. Drac doesn't look so impressed," he said.

Murray agreed with Crystal. "Man, this is amazing! There's so much to do. Olympic-sized swimming pool!"

A monster dove into the pool.

"All-you-can-eat buffet!" Murray was excited.

A skeleton picked up the entire table and gobbled the food, table and all. He burped. One of the fish crew members popped back out of his mouth.

"Full-service spa!" Murray pointed out.

Through the spa window, Bigfoot was on a massage

table with three fish crew members giving him a massage.

"Oooooo! I'm gonna get me a seaweed rewrap!" Murray said.

Drac groaned and said sarcastically, "Wow. It sounds like everything we can do at our hotel."

"Except on the water," Murray corrected.

Suddenly fireworks exploded above them. Dennis flew past Mavis and Johnny, who were holding Winnie.

"Wow!" Dennis yelled happily.

Johnny leaned over to Mavis and said, "You nailed it, honey! Your dad is going to love this! Best summer vacation ever!"

Mavis nodded. "Wait till you see the itinerary," she hinted.

Even Frank liked the fireworks. Usually fire terrified him!

"Ohhh, that's nice," Frank said, admiring the show.

Dracula was confused. "Frank, 'fire bad,' remember?" he said, mimicking what Frank usually said when he saw a flame.

"Oh yeah, right, but uh . . . Maybe you'll find your

own fireworks on the cruise? Huh?" Frank asked.

"It's not the Love Boat, Frank," Drac said. "I'm just here to have fun with my family."

Suddenly an energetic figure swung through the crowd, catching Drac's attention. The woman landed on a mast above everyone.

The crowd cheered as she welcomed the international monsters, being super friendly.

"Ahoy there! Welcome aboard! *Bienvenido! Willkommen! Dobro pozalovat! Huānyíng!*" It was impressive how many languages she knew. The woman even greeted Bigfoot by saying, "Wreeeerrraaarrooorr!"

Bigfoot roared back, delighted. "Wrrrooorr!"

Murray asked Drac, "Whoa! Who is that?"

But Drac didn't answer. A familiar purple zing cast itself over his face, and Drac couldn't take his eyes off this woman.

"I am Captain Ericka," she said to the crowd. "And yes, I'm human, but don't hold it against me! I could not be more excited to have all of you on board our first-ever monster cruise!"

The monsters cheered.

Drac was now sweating, and his heart was beating fast and loud! He was singularly focused on Ericka.

Mavis was cheering and laughing, until she noticed Drac's expression. "Dad, uh, are you okay?"

"Ina finny, fanny! Oh no wa-wa." He muttered some gibberish.

Mavis stared at her dad, then got concerned. "Oh no! He's having a heart attack!"

Murray looked over. "Drac? Not likely."

"Yeah, the only heart attack that can hurt him is with a wooden stake," Wayne said.

Mavis waved her hand in front of her dad's face. "It must be a stroke!"

Wayne glanced at Drac, then noticed where he was looking. "Actually, I think it might be her." He pointed to Ericka, but accidentally poked the Invisible Man in the eye with his finger.

"Ow!" Griffin exclaimed. "Watch where you're pointing, mister! I'm right here."

Wayne shook his head and said, "You always stand so close to me. It's creepy."

Ericka gracefully slid down the mast onto the deck.

41

"For so long, monsters were hiding, living in the shadows. But not anymore! You stood up and waved your hand, or claw, or tentacle, and said, 'We're here, we're hairy, and it is our right to be scary!'"

The monsters were really into it. Everyone cheered!

The captain went on. "Now it's time to celebrate! You'll enjoy gourmet dining, thrilling adventures, and nonstop entertainment, all on the way to our final destination, the lost city that isn't lost anymore . . . Atlantis!"

The crowd went wild. They went even crazier when the doors behind Captain Ericka swung open and the fish crew performed a circus of acrobatics and amazing tricks.

"Oh, yeah!" Dennis shouted.

"Woo-hoo!" Winnie exclaimed. Then she and Dennis ran off to watch with Johnny and Mavis.

Ericka walked around, greeting people one by one. "Hello. How y'all doing?" She caught Drac staring at her and approached him. "So, you must be the one and only Dracula."

Dracula gulped.

"I have waited SO long to meet you." Ericka leaned

in so close that her breath touched his face. "Wow, you really don't age, do you? I would kill for your skin."

Dracula mumbled something, and drooled a little, but couldn't speak. It came out as, "Eh . . . Doobie-day-shu-la koobie day."

Ericka was confused at first, but then her eyes lit up. "Ooh! You're speaking Transylvanian. I've always wanted to learn." She repeated what he'd said, "Doobie-day-shu-la koobie day."

Drac tried again to make himself understood, but they ended up going back and forth like someone practicing with language tapes.

"Koobie-day." He struggled with words.

"Koobie-day?" Ericka repeated.

Drac was growing frustrated with himself. "Koobie-day!"

She echoed him. "Koobie-day!"

It just got worse. Drac said, "Doola-day-shu-la koobie day."

And she said back, "Doola-day-shu-la koobie day." Ericka had no idea what it all meant. "Ahh, such a romantic language. You know, there's just something about an accent that makes a man sound so intelligent."

Dracula blushed and said, "Ali-booboo."

Finally, Frank stepped in to rescue Drac. "That's Transylvanian right there. He's saying, 'It was nice to meet you.'"

With that, Frank dragged Drac away before he could embarrass himself even more.

Ericka waved at them. "Well then, ali-booboo to you as well." She watched Drac leave.

In a hidden corner of the ship's deck, Frank, Wayne, Murray, and Griffin tried to force the vampire back to reality.

"Alibooboo, aaalibooboo, alibooboo, alibooboo," Drac mumbled.

"Drac! Drac! Snap out of it!" Frank shook him.

"Alibooboo," Drac replied.

"Wait, wait." Griffin had a plan. "I've always wanted to do this." He threw his glass of champagne into Drac's face and started gently slapping his cheeks to try to bring him to his senses. "Wake up! Wake up, Drac! Snap out of it!"

"Hey! Cut it out!" Frank stopped Griffin as Drac pulled himself together.

"Hey, buddy, you okay?" Frank asked Drac.

"No, no, not okay, not okay," Drac admitted.

The guys looked at Drac. They were concerned.

"I . . . I . . . I . . . zinged."

CHAPTER FIVE

It was the first night at sea. Everyone gathered to hear the fish man band play. In addition to dancing, other activities were happening all around the boat. Outside, a group of old witch ladies lounged by the pool. One of the witches tipped her sunglasses and took a look at a man who was humming to himself.

It was Drac's father, Vlad, wearing a swimsuit. "It's a lovely day today," he cooed.

The witches popped up from their lounging positions and gawked.

"Ooo!"

"Ohh!"

"Check that out!"

Vlad chuckled and puffed up his chest to look like a vampire who enjoyed the gym.

"Ahhh. He he eh ahhh . . . Here we go . . ." He set his towel down onto a chair.

The witches came to sit with him.

"Mmm," one witch said.

"Yummy," the second agreed.

"Grrr," the third witch flirted.

Vlad wiggled his tummy, did some stretches, and settled into his chair. "Eyy ohh, oop, ahhh . . ." He was ready to enjoy the evening.

On deck, Blobby leaned against the railing, seasick. He turned multiple colors until he finally threw up . . . a little blob. The baby blob happily hugged his parent, Blobby, saying, "Blubluh."

Meanwhile, Wayne and Wanda were walking across the deck with all their crying and rowdy pups when they discovered a doorway with a sign that said KIDS CLUB. Wanda gasped.

"Kids club? What's a kids club?" Wayne wondered.

When they peeked in, they saw monster kids having fun. A monster slid down a kiddy slide. "Weee!" He hit the bottom a little hard, but laughed.

A fish man kids club worker picked up the kid and put him in a kiddie pen with other monster kids.

Wayne didn't understand what was going on. He went inside, still wearing a bunch of the young ones in multiple baby carriers.

"Fish!" Sunny declared.

"That's right, dear," Wanda said, shushing Sunny.

"I'm still not sure I understand," Wayne told the kids club worker, who was at the sign-in desk. "You take my kids, all day, on purpose?"

"Fish!" Sunny said again.

"That's right!" the fish man said, wanting to help. "What exactly don't you understand?"

"Why?" Wayne asked. Then he howled, "Owww!" when Wanda elbowed him in the ribs.

"So they can have a great time and *you* can have a great time," the fish man explained.

"Fish!" Sunny shouted even louder this time.

Wayne started crying tears of joy.

Now it was the fish man who didn't understand. He thought Wayne was honestly sad. "Don't worry. You get them back at the end of the day."

That was disappointing, and Wayne's face fell a little bit.

"Fish," Sunny said again.

"Oh, well. It's better than nothing," Wayne said. He gave a soft wolf whistle, and the fish man's jaw dropped as the wolf pups rushed in, knocking over the grown-ups.

Wayne and Wanda left the club alone, stunned at their good fortune.

Behind them, on the other side of the glass doors, the wolf pups were already making a mess.

Wayne smiled at his wife. "So, what do we do now?"

"I think . . . I think . . . we do whatever we want?" Wanda said, but she wasn't sure what she wanted to do.

"Whatever . . . we . . . want," Wayne cheered.

"Whatever . . . we . . . . want," Wanda repeated.

Wayne and Wanda grew giant maniacal grins as they understood that they were free!

Wayne sang, "Whatever we want! Whatever we want! Whatever we want!"

Wanda sang too. "Whatever we want! Whatever we want! Whatever we want!"

Wayne said, "Whatever we want!"

"Whatever we want!" Wanda was so excited.

In the kids club, Stan tried to escape from the pups, crawling to the door while shouting, "Aaah! Nooo! Stop! Help me! Noooooo!" But he was dragged back inside by the little monsters.

"Welcome aboard." Captain Ericka greeted Harry Three-Eye before sneaking past him into a hidden passageway.

Down below, in the bowels of the cruise ship, Ericka snuck into a secretive-looking doorway and made her way down into a hidden stateroom. The room was dark and old, with wood paneling. On the walls were framed clippings and old photographs of Van Helsing and his exploits.

"Ugh," Ericka said to a shadowed figure in the room. "You were so right, Great-grandfather. Monsters are disgusting."

The real Van Helsing, the oldest man in the world, replied, "They're animals." He rolled into the light. His wheelchair was steam operated, with a machine that helped him breathe. "Dracula . . . is he on board?"

"Yes," Ericka assured him. "I saw him, face-to-face. Ugh. I was nice to him!" As she spoke, she tightened a bolt on Van Helsing's wheelchair. "With that pale face of his and goofy smile, showing off his fangs. He was looking at my neck like it was corn on the cob. It's just like you taught me."

Van Helsing was upset. "It's even worse than I feared. The world is falling apart. Monsters mixing with people. People mixing with monsters. Where does it end?"

Ericka flipped over Van Helsing, spinning and landing on the other side of him. "Let me get rid of Dracula right now! I was so close to him, I could have just—" She grabbed a blade and pushed it, hard, into a wood table.

"No!" Van Helsing tugged a chain on his wheelchair, which let out a loud steam whistle, interrupting her. "He's too powerful. If I couldn't defeat him in my prime, how could you even stand a chance?" He paused, thinking back to long ago. "It was that fateful night that I realized a human could never defeat Dracula."

Van Helsing remembered a room full of portraits of old Van Helsing family members going back generations. He had stood in front of that original Van Helsing and yelled, "Why? Why? Why did you pass this legacy down to me? To make me look like a fool?" He kicked the bottom of the giant portrait with his tiny boot—and the whole thing fell on top of him.

He looked through books in the Van Helsing Library. "I dug deep in the annals of history.... Then I saw it ... in an ancient text ... the ultimate device! So powerful, it destroyed Atlantis, a whole city of monsters." The device was still in the rubble of Atlantis. Van Helsing had used an old map to Atlantis's location, hoping to find it.

"Thus began my quest," he said. "Endlessly, I searched for the lost city. Time passed and my body began to fail me, but my genius persevered! I replaced my failing organs with their mechanical equivalents. And now after a hundred and twenty years I have finally found Atlantis and the device that lies within!"

Ericka was still focused on killing Drac. "Right, but can't I just—" she tried.

Van Helsing snapped. "We have to stick to the plan. Lure the monsters to Atlantis and then use the device to destroy them all. Now, promise me you won't try to kill Dracula," he ordered.

"Fine, I promise," Ericka said.

"Promise what?" he nudged, giving her a stern look.

Ericka gave in and blurted, "I-promise-I-won't-try-to-kill-Dracula. Okay?"

Relieved, Van Helsing leaned back and smiled. The "nap meter" dial on his chair moved to full blast. He immediately fell asleep and began to snore.

That's when Ericka whispered softly, "Don't worry, Great-grandfather. I won't try to kill him. I *will* kill him."

CHAPTER SIX

Drac left his cabin wearing new cabana clothes: a skull-and-flowers-themed Hawaiian shirt, white short shorts, black knee-high dress socks, and white loafers. He still had that goofy "I'm in love" smile as he started to dance through the ship.

As she emerged from the secret entrance, Ericka noticed Drac strutting along happily.

She saw there was an emergency flare on the wall nearby and got an idea.

While she took down the flare, Drac ran into Blobby, who jiggled while joining him in his fun jaunt across the deck.

As the two moved, side by side, Ericka was hidden behind a small vent with the flare. She took dead aim on Drac and fired. But as luck would have it, Drac sidestepped as part of his happy-go-lucky stride. The flare missed him and hit Blobby instead. The flare exploded inside of the blobby body. Blobby inflated and then deflated, not noticing that anything unusual had happened.

"Grrr!" Ericka grumbled, but then she spied a life-boat above Drac's head. She quickly pulled a lever, which caused the boat to drop hard right onto Blobby, because Drac moved out of the way of a stampede of wolf pups just in time.

Blobby regained his shape but still had the lifeboat stuck in him, and continued happily strutting with Drac. Ericka was growing frustrated. This wasn't as easy as she'd imagined.

Some boat workmen were operating a crane, lifting supplies. Ericka commandeered the crane and sunk the heavy supplies right into Blobby, just missing Drac because he walked to the railing to see some dolphins jumping out of the water. Blobby was clobbered and launched off the boat.

Underwater, Blobby hit the propeller, and then bounced back out of the water, right back on top of Drac.

Ericka couldn't believe this was happening to her! She slunk away as Drac and Blobby passed the pool.

Drac began to strut.

"Work it, Dracula!" Mavis told her dad.

"You know it." Drac struck a wild pose, fists pumped.

"Oo, looking good, Drac," Frank said.

"Feeling good, Frank." Drac swung into another pose. This time with his arms crossed.

"Look at you, so fancy," Eunice complimented.

Dracula showed off his outfit. "What? This? Please."

"Oo, dressed to impress, huh?" Murray put in.

"Impress? Oh, who do I need to impress?" Drac swayed to the music.

"Hey, isn't that Captain Ericka?" Griffin pointed over Drac's back.

Drac instantly spun around and peeked, then tried to hide under the deck chair pillow.

"Ohhh! No, no! Wa Do Da Di! Ah ehh ooooh," Drac mumbled.

"Oops, no, not her," Griffin laughed.

All the monsters found it funny, but Drac was a mess. He slumped onto a deck chair. "Hehe . . . Yes, yes, very amusing . . . Uhh ah . . . he, he . . ."

The guys felt bad.

Frank said, "Sorry, Drac. You know it's just that we've never seen you like this."

"I know." Dracula found his voice. "It doesn't make any sense. You can't zing twice. It's impossible. But I did, so now what?" He realized that he wasn't sure how his daughter would feel about her dad falling for someone other than her mother. "And what about Mavis?"

"She wants you to be happy, right?" Murray asked. "I'm sure she'll go with the flow."

Drac wasn't so sure. "Oh no. Mavis needs me. She depends on me. I need to be home with my family."

Griffin joked, "Murray here may be from Egypt, but you're the one in de-*nial*."

Drac didn't laugh. Instead, he elbowed Griffin. Then they saw Mavis coming toward them.

"Mavis!" Drac yelled to his daughter, and then turned to his friends and hissed a warning under his breath. "Don't say a word, or I'll haunt your dreams!"

The threat worked.

"Having fun?" Mavis asked her dad, casually.

"I'm having even more fun now that you're here," Drac replied as if nothing interesting was up.

Mavis said, "You know, Dad, I feel really lucky to have this time with you. All of us together. It's really special."

Drac cast an I-told-you-so glance at his friends, then said, "Me too, spider monkey."

"Now, ready for me to destroy you in monsterball? Dennis and Johnny are already in the pool."

"Come on, Papa Drac!" Dennis shouted.

"Oh ho, bring it on, for I AM KING OF ALL BALLS!" Drac said, and everyone laughed.

The gang all got into the pool. It was Mavis, Dennis, Drac, Johnny, and Murray on one side, and Frank, Eunice, Vlad, Griffin, and Crystal on the other side.

Murray took the volleyball first and was ready to serve. "All right, who is ready to get pummeled?"

Vlad mocked Murray's team, saying, "Ooh. I'm shaking in my trunks."

"I'm not wearing any trunks. Hehehe," Griffin shared with them all.

"Ewwwwwwwwww." Eunice shook off the image of Griffin naked.

"I gotta warn you, I played second-team coed intramural volleyball at Santa Cruz." Johnny did some funny stretches, including a double armpit toot.

"Sure, pal. Whatever you say." Frank was ready to play.

Eunice had one rule. "Everybody, just please, watch the hair, watch the hair."

"Let's do this. Let's do this!" Drac got into position.

Mavis was so happy to see her dad having a good time. "Oh my gosh, this is going to be so much fun!"

Ericka was hiding nearby, watching in disgust as the monsters began their game.

"Get ready! Here comes the paaaaaaain!" Murray was about to serve. The mummy lobbed the ball up and served it hard over the net, straight at Vlad.

Vlad hit it hard. "OYE!" And it went over to Eunice.

"Not the hair! Not the hair!" she screamed, before hitting it over the net.

Johnny screamed as it passed over his head.

Mavis dove to get the ball and hit it super high. "Dad, all yours!"

Drac hit the ball over the net to Eunice, who missed it. The splash soaked her hair, causing it to get frizzy.

Drac's team cheered!

The ship's whistle blew, and a fish man voice made a ship-wide announcement.

"Captain Ericka, you are needed on deck."

She was still hiding out of the sight of the players, but that announcement gave Ericka an idea.

Back in the game, Murray had the ball and served it well. It went to Vlad, who started his spooky scream, scaring the ball back the other way.

"Ahhhhhhhhh!" Vlad chuckled at his power.

The ball was above Mavis, who bumped it over the net right to Frank, who spiked it back, straight to Drac. He was about to hit it, when Ericka turned on a microphone so she could make an announcement of her own.

"I got this . . . ," Drac started to say. He was moving toward the ball as if in slow motion, when he heard a voice.

"Hey there, monsters!" Ericka said nearby, her voice echoing over the PA system.

That voice was all it took to distract Drac. Instantly Drac turned to look at Ericka, and the ball landed on his head and stuck there!

"Woo-hoo! What I say!" Frank celebrated that he had scored a point.

"We're arriving at our first destination," Ericka said, when suddenly there was a huge explosion of water. "The underwater volcano!"

They had made it, but they had no idea what Ericka had in store for them.

"Ooh!" the crowd cheered.

"Everyone, grab your scuba gear and get ready to explore the wonders of the sea," Ericka said. Then, looking at Drac as he struggled to get the monsterball off his head, Ericka called out to him. "Especially you, Count Dracula."

Drac looked surprised.

Mavis noticed his expression, paused for a second, and then shrugged it off as nothing. She headed out of the pool to get ready.

When she was gone, Frank leaned over to Drac. "See that, pal? She likes you."

"No, no, no," Drac protested.

"That sounds like a zing in full effect," Murray agreed.

"No, no, no," Drac said again.

"Yes, yes, yes," Griffin said.

Drac pushed them all aside. "I'm just here to have family fun," he insisted. Then he went to get ready to go diving.

CHAPTER SEVEN

First, a twelve-eyed monster put on twelve scuba masks and dove into the water.

Then Bigfoot headed in wearing giant flippers.

No one noticed as Ericka got into a secret vessel, turned it on, and loaded it with wooden stakes.

Unaware, Johnny, Dennis, Mavis, and Drac were soon decked out in their scuba gear, trying to walk on deck with flippers on their feet.

When the monsters were ready, everyone jumped off the deck, plummeting down into the giant volcano.

A brightly colored coral reef surrounded the volcano's crater, where red lava flowed slowly into the water.

The monsters' guide was Stan, the fish man, and he could effortlessly talk underwater. "Welcome to Volcano del Fuego. Please follow me to explore a rare kelp forest, home to stingrays, sea horses, and my cousin." He led the way, and everyone eagerly followed.

The monsters were so busy exploring that they didn't notice when a fish-shaped submarine floated out of an opening near the bottom of the cruise ship. Ericka was inside, and she was trying to catch up with Drac so she could get rid of him, once and for all.

While the monsters were checking out the lava pools, Ericka spotted Drac and pedaled toward him.

Dennis and Drac swam around and ran into a shark. Dennis panicked, but not for long, because Drac hypnotized the shark. They jumped onto its back as if it were a horse and galloped along in the ocean, behind Ericka's ship-in-disguise.

Drac was having a ball. Then he saw a seahorse swim by and began to copy its movements by wiggling his body. Dennis and Winnie giggled with delight! Then they tried to move like a seahorse too. Soon even Johnny and Mavis joined in the fun!

Ericka had steered her submarine behind a coral reef and wanted to try to hit Drac. When she saw Drac pretending to be a seahorse, she couldn't help but giggle. She tried to stay focused on her mission and tried to hit Drac with wooden harpoons, but missed. Instead, the harpoons hit a bunch of manta rays who'd swum between her and Drac just in time!

Drac began to imitate the manta rays, too. Soon hundreds of fish swam by, and Drac followed them to Ericka's submarine. It looked a lot like a real fish, so he thought it was just another fish in the school.

Ericka tried to steer the submarine away from Drac, but he grabbed ahold of its tail. He was pretending to capture it and asked Mavis to take a photo of him with his "catch."

Ericka panicked, took a huge breath, and launched herself out the submarine's escape hatch.

Mavis took the photo of Drac, and in the corner of the image she could have sworn she spotted two human feet. She thought she must be imagining it. . . .

When Ericka reached the surface of the water, she coughed violently. She reached the ship's submarine dock, not realizing that Frank, Murray, and Griffin were swimming nearby. They had been exploring an underwater cave but came back to the ship to get a snack.

When they reached the ship, they started going up the stairs to get food, when they overheard Ericka muttering, "Dracula! Dracula! Dracula!" and froze, trying not to make a sound. Ericka went on. "I get so close, but it's almost like he's teasing me. I can't stand it anymore. . . . I have to get him!" she exclaimed, stomping her foot.

The guys thought Ericka had romantic thoughts about Drac, but she actually was still trying to kill him! They hurried away to find Drac to tell him that Ericka seemed to like him, too!

Back on deck, everyone changed out of their scuba gear. Drac, Mavis, Johnny, and Dennis were drying off when they saw Tinkles, still wearing his disguise, but whining at Dennis as if he had missed his friend during the scuba excursion.

Mavis stared at the beast, who looked very familiar. "Um, Dennis, who is this?"

Dennis said quickly, "Oh, it's our friend Bob."

"Say 'hi,' Bob," Winnie instructed Tinkles.

"Hi, Bob," the dog repeated.

"Okay, time to go play Ping-Pong!" Dennis declared.

Johnny liked that idea. "Ooh, I'm in! Pro tip: call it table tennis."

Dennis had to protect Bob's identity. "Uh, sorry, Dad. There's no room."

Dennis and Winnie ushered Bob away as everyone stared at them, watching them go.

Johnny was undeterred. "How about some foosball? Air hockey?!" he called out, but the kids were gone.

Just then, Frank, Murray, and Griffin came running across the deck, knocking monsters and waiters over.

"Drac! Drac! Drac!" their voices rang in a chorus.

When they noticed Mavis standing next to Drac, they slowed, knowing he wouldn't want Mavis to know anything about Ericka.

"Hey, boys, where's the fire?" Dracula asked, squinting at them with curiosity.

"Oh, uh, well," Frank stammered, staring at Mavis. "Griffin here wanted to uh—"

"Yeah, he had something to tell ya—" Murray started.

They both looked at Griffin for the answer. "Me?! Oh, uh, yeah, see . . . I got this bite on my hand, and since, you know, you're a biting expert, I thought you could take a look." It wasn't a good excuse, but it was something.

"Yeah, c'mon over here," they told Drac, calling him away from Mavis.

"The light is better," Murray said.

Mavis watched them as they all walked away. She had a feeling something was up.

The guys shuffled Drac to a private place around a corner.

"Okay, what is going on? You guys are acting weirder than normal, and your normal is pretty weird," Drac said.

"You are not gonna believe what we heard—" Frank started, but was interrupted when Murray began singing.

"Ericka loves the Drac. She can't get enough of the Drac. Oh yeah, Drac is back. He's got the zinnnng—" Murray belted out.

Dracula put up a hand. "Shhhh! I told you I don't want

68

to upset Mavis." He realized what his friends were saying and added, "But what are you talking about?"

Griffin started the story. "Well, see, Frank got hungry, no surprise, and we swam back to the ship and found Ericka raving about you."

"She can't live without you, buddy," Frank added. "It's *serious*."

"You can't deny the zing, baby," Murray told him.

Just then, Ericka stepped onto the deck. Noticing them talking, she quickly hid so that she could listen in on their conversation.

"So, Drac, you going to make a move on the captain or what?" Griffin asked.

"Yes . . . Maybe? . . . No. Ah, it's been a while. I don't even know where to start," Drac admitted with growing frustration.

Hearing this, Ericka was grossed out at first, but then she had a brilliant idea.

"It's easy, Drac. Just make some small talk," Murray suggested.

"Remember to smile," Griffin suggested.

"Look into her eyes," Frank said.

"Keep it casual," Murray told Drac.

"Say something funny," Griffin said.

"Ask her where her parts are from?" Frank smiled.

"Oh, and say that her wrappings look nice!" Murray smoothed his own wrappings.

"Do you like coffins?" Griffin thought that was a good one.

"Compliment her: Say 'your neck looks delicious.'" Frank laughed at his own advice.

Drac was speechless. As he stood there, like a deer in headlights, Ericka walked in as if she had just arrived.

"Okay, Drac, hit it." Griffin spun Drac around and shoved him face-to-face with Ericka.

It took him a second to get started, but then he said nervously, "Your delicious neck wrappings are in the nice coffin. Would you like to see my parts?"

It was awful. The guys winced.

Griffin imitated the sound of an airplane crashing and burning. "Fwuuuuuuuuuuuuu . . . kerprrrr!"

But then Ericka answered Dracula, saying, "Yes, I'd love to go out with you."

Dracula was stunned. He couldn't believe his ears. "What?" he asked.

"Cantina. Midnight. Don't be late," Ericka said coolly, and then left the deck.

Dracula smiled goofily as he watched her go.

CHAPTER EIGHT

The ship sailed through the night until it reached a classic-looking little island with a few palm trees.

The fish man announced their evening activity. "Hey, everybody! We are at our next stop, the 'Deserted Island.'" As he spoke, the ship docked next to a resort island.

Down on the lower deck, monster passengers lined up to go to the shore.

Johnny was holding a mountain of toys, towels, chairs, sunscreen, and more, but it didn't seem to bother him. "Woo-hoo! Beach time!" he said happily.

"Johnny, you go set everything up," Mavis said, and

then turned to Drac. "Dad, you go get in line for the snow cones."

"You know, actually, I was thinking you and Johnny should spend some time together. What do you call it again? Date night?" Drac told her.

Johnny dropped the huge pile of beach stuff. "Date night?" It sounded great to him!

"What are you going to do?" Mavis asked.

"Well, I thought me and the guys would take this opportunity to spend some one-on-one, quality time with Dennis," Dracula told her.

Mavis smiled. "Oh, okay. That's a great idea! Come on, Johnny!"

Johnny pumped his fist and cheered, "Date night!"

A short time later, the cruise ship monsters were enjoying the beach. Blobby and baby Blobby set up their space under the bright rays of the moonlight. They cut pieces of themselves and made blob umbrellas before settling down.

Wayne and Wanda played fetch like actual dogs. Their game was interrupted by a roar of cries . . . and barks.

"What was that?" Wayne asked.

"It sounds like our children," Wanda said sadly.

"It *is* our children!" Wayne yelled.

Wanda told him to run just as the fish man from the kids club yelled out, "For the love of COD! Someone get the parents!"

Meanwhile, Frank and Eunice were enjoying the heat, but needed to reapply the sunscreen.

"Frank, rub some sunscreen on my back before I get burned," Eunice told her husband.

"Oh, one second, honey. The kids buried me in the sand." Unfortunately, Winnie and Dennis had buried pieces of him all over the place. One arm hopped over to Eunice and started rubbing the lotion onto her back.

In a nearby restaurant with a deserted-island theme, Johnny's face glowed in the flickering light of a candle.

"Isn't this place amazing?" he asked Mavis. "Wow! The menu is in a bottle. Isn't that awesome, honey?"

Mavis was too distracted to notice. "What? Oh, sorry. I was just thinking about my dad. Don't you think he's been acting weird lately?"

"Not really," Johnny said, keeping his eye on the chef, "besides having a huge crush on the captain."

Those words blew Mavis away! "What?" she asked Johnny. She'd had no idea her dad liked the captain.

"Oh yeah. The Love Boat is definitely making another run," Johnny said, and laughed.

"No way. He's"—she paused, then said—"my dad."

"I know, right? It's weird. When my parents kiss, I still close my eyes." Johnny gagged.

"I guess I never thought about him with any-one besides my mom," Mavis said, considering the possibility.

"You're cool with it, though, right?" Johnny asked.

"Of course. I want him to be happy," Mavis said.

"Totally," Johnny added.

On board, in the ship's cantina, the restaurant was romantic and dimly lit. Fish men crew members played in a mariachi band and served up drinks.

Ericka, looking stunning in a fiesta dress, walked over to Drac.

"Good evening. You look ravishing," he told her.

"Oh, thank you. I just . . ." That particular compliment made Ericka uncomfortable.

Drac magically pulled out a chair for her, and they sat down.

Drac started the conversation. "So does Captain Ericka have a last name?"

Ericka got nervous for a second, then blurted out, "Guacamole!"

"Ericka Guacamole?" Drac asked. "That's so . . . international."

"No. I ordered guacamole for us to share," she said. The waiter brought in the guac and set it on the table. Ericka tried to distract Drac. "Oh, how beautiful is that full moon tonight?" she asked.

While Drac was distracted, Ericka took out her vial of highly concentrated garlic oil and dumped the whole thing into the guacamole. She'd been taught that garlic was deadly for vampires like Drac.

"Mmm. The food here is to die for," Ericka said.

Then she took a chip from the basket, dunked it in the guacamole, and fed it to Drac. "Mmm," she said.

"Mmm hhhm hmmm mmm," Drac agreed, swallowing hard.

Ericka took another chip covered in guacamole and fed it again to Dracula. "MMMmmm," she said.

"MMM MM HMMM HMM," he said.

Ericka took two more chips loaded with guacamole and fed them to Drac. And then two more chips! Drac's mouth was completely full with chips and guac. He swallowed again.

"Holy moly that was a lot of guacamole," Drac said, glancing at the bowl.

"Are you feeling all right?" Ericka asked. She had honestly thought he'd be dead by now.

"Totally fine. Why?" Drac asked.

"No reason." Ericka didn't understand why he wasn't dead yet! Garlic killed vampires, right?

Drac's tummy suddenly grumbled, loudly.

"Oh. I wonder if there was garlic in the guacamole?" Drac asked.

"I don't know," Ericka lied. Then she looked at him closely. "Isn't that deadly for you?"

"No," Dracula told her. "It's just that I'm intolerant . . ." With that, Drac let out a toot! He began to sweat, and an embarrassed grin spread over his face. "Hehe, was that you?" Drac said.

Out on the beach, Mavis and Johnny walked back toward the ship in the moonlight, hand in hand.

"Woah!" Johnny said, noticing a cool sand castle.

The gang had built a giant sand castle that looked exactly like Hotel Transylvania! It was big enough that they all fit inside.

"Hi, Momma! Hi, Papa!" Dennis said, jumping out of the sand castle.

"Hey, hey!" said Winnie.

Then Murray, Blobby, baby Blobby, and Frank popped out.

"Is my dad in there too?" Mavis asked.

Everyone hopped back inside the sand castle . . . and then a voice from inside said, "Don't worry. I'm over here, blah blah blah." It didn't sound like Drac at all, because it was Griffin pretending to be Drac.

Then Dennis spilled the beans, not realizing it was a secret. "No, he's not. He's on his—"

Before he could finish, Mavis finished his sentence. "Date?" she asked.

Back in the cantina, Ericka was still upset that her plan to kill Drac hadn't worked. And Drac was mortified by his gassiness.

"Please forgive me," he said. "I'm just very nervous. You see, I haven't had a date since my wife died." He paused awkwardly.

Ericka slightly softened, ready to listen. "How old was your daughter?"

"She was just an infant. That's why I opened the hotel, so that I could stay at home and raise her. I did my best."

His story touched Ericka, who became quiet and reflective.

"I never knew my mother either, or my father," she revealed to him.

"I'm so sorry," he said, full of concern. "Who raised you?"

"My great-grandfather," Ericka said. "I basically grew up on this ship." There was a hint of regret in her voice.

"That's why you're a captain," Drac said, processing her story.

"Yeah, it's all I've ever known. It was just expected. You know, a family thing," she explained.

"I understand. Family is everything." Dracula got it. "You have to honor the past. But we make our own future."

Drac had no idea he had hit on something Ericka had been struggling with. She didn't want to be on the boat forever. She wanted to make her own future, and he understood.

CHAPTER NINE

Then Mavis walked in.

"Dad?" Mavis asked, surprised to see him with Ericka.

"Mavis! Johnny!" Drac said. He was surprised to see them too.

Because of the interruption, Ericka had a change of heart about Drac. She became very self-conscious about the fact that she had almost lost sight of her true mission. "This is a bad idea. I'm sorry. I have to go." She stood up and prepared to leave.

"Ericka . . ." Drac rose. He didn't want the evening to end like this.

Johnny could now see Drac and Ericka's table, and he felt guilty for bringing Mavis into the cantina . . . but he got over it and grabbed some chips and guacamole from Drac's table.

Drac started to explain to Mavis why he was eating dinner with Ericka, but he made up a story, and he wasn't a very good liar. "Captain Ericka and I were just discussing the hospitality industry! You know, work stuff."

Ericka nodded.

Mavis was not buying the story but didn't want to confront him or deal with what was really happening. "You're working now? This is supposed to be a vacation. A family vacation," she said.

"I should really go do captain-y things." Ericka headed to the door and left as fast as she could.

Mavis turned back to Dracula. "Dad, you said you were going to spend time with Dennis."

"You're right! Where is that kid? Dennis? Denisovich, you're supposed to be with me. Come on, now, kid. It's family time!" Drac called out.

Drac hurried out of the cantina.

Concerned, Mavis turned to Johnny, who wasn't worried

at all. "What was that about?" Mavis asked her husband.

"You mean your dad's date?" Johnny asked her.

"It wasn't a date! It was work," Mavis insisted.

"Uh-huh . . ." Johnny let her believe what she wanted.

"I'm telling you, Johnny, there's something about that woman I don't trust," Mavis said, feeling as if she had a stone in her belly.

"But you want your dad to be happy, right?" Johnny asked her.

"Yes." Mavis sighed.

Johnny smiled, happy that he'd convinced her, and then ate another chip loaded with guac.

"Just not with her," Mavis muttered.

"Heads up, honey!" Johnny said, still focused on the guac. "This guac is loaded with garlic!" He grabbed a sip of Drac's drink to wash it down.

"Garlic?" Mavis asked. Then she tried it too. Immediately her stomach rumbled and the tiniest little toot came out.

"Aw, that was a cute toot, honey." Johnny grinned.

Mavis narrowed her eyes. She was now more suspicious about Ericka than ever.

83

Wayne and Wanda were on the deck, running around and jumping onto lifeboats and having a great time.

Wanda was still so grateful to be on the cruise with her husband while the fish men watched the pups. "We've been up all night!" she said.

"Let's stay up all day, too!" Wayne suggested with a chuckle.

"Let's get wild," Wanda agreed.

They howled together, and then ran off on all fours, happy and carefree.

Ericka stepped back to stay out of sight as Wayne and Wanda ran by. She stood against a wall. Behind her, Van Helsing's head popped out of a ship's vent.

"Ericka!" Van Helsing surprised her.

She screamed. "Ahhh! What?"

"Just where have you been, young lady?" her great-grandfather asked.

"Doing work," Ericka told the old man.

"You were with *him*. I know it!" Van Helsing said, accusing her.

Ericka played dumb. "Who?"

"You know who," Van Helsing said in a raised voice that echoed. "You've been sneaking around behind my back trying to kill Dracula, haven't you?"

"So what if I have?" Ericka asked. "I'm a grown woman. I have the right to kill whoever I want."

"It's not just about you. You could have ruined the legacy. What if he discovered who you were?"

Ericka sighed. She was completely confused. "I know! I know! I wasn't thinking. There's just something about him that drives me crazy! I see him and I want to—"

"Punch him," Van Helsing said sympathetically.

"I guess," Ericka told him. "I just can't wait to get this over with." But that wasn't the whole truth.

"Don't worry. It won't be long now. Once you recover the device, no one can stop us . . . not even Dracula," Van Helsing assured her.

Just then, Wayne and Wanda burst around the corner, howling happily.

Wayne looked casually around the room, then said, "Oh. 'Scuse me."

"Spies!" Van Helsing accused them. He quickly

blew tranquilizer darts at Wayne and Wanda. They both fell to the deck, unconscious.

Ericka and her great-grandfather dragged Wayne and Wanda down to Van Helsing's rooms, where they stuffed the couple into a closet, still asleep from the darts.

Dracula was coming out of his stateroom, when there was an announcement.

"Everyone, please assemble on the forward deck. We are about to arrive at our final destination: the greatest monster civilization the world has ever known, surpassing Athens and Rome in art, culture, and sophistication. I give you the legendary lost city of Atlantis."

As they approached, giant tentacles surrounded the boat and startled Johnny.

It was the Kraken, a legendary sea monster and lounge singer. And it began to sing:

There's a place you've gotta be,
A thousand leagues beneath the sea,
And it's waiting over here for you
and me ...

With a sweep of his hand, the fish man directed everyone to look out as Atlantis came into view.

Atlantis was like Las Vegas for monsters. It was glittery with bright lights.

When the ship docked, the monsters' path to the Atlantis casino was lit with spotlights and lined with giant statues. Laser light shows turned waterfalls rainbow colors, and everything sparkled. The monsters approached a casino that looked like a giant aquarium, with whales swimming through the walls, ceiling, and floor. There was even a roller coaster!

In the center was a giant statue of King Triton. The animatronic ruler greeted the monsters as they came in, saying, "Welcome to Atlantis!"

The monsters quickly settled in and started gambling.

A monster went to a row of slot machines and used all of her tentacles to pull five levers at once . . . and hit the jackpot on the first try!

Frank took out a wad of cash and set it on a card table. "Oooh, I am so excited!"

"Oh, no you don't!" Eunice told him, and then picked up the cash and waved it at Frank. "Last time

87

you played cards, you lost an arm and a leg . . . literally."

Frank wasn't listening. Without using his neck, his eyes rotated to the back of his head to watch the poker game!

"Replacement limbs aren't just lying around like they were in the old days, so no gambling! FRANK!" Eunice demanded.

Frank's eyes zipped back to the front of his head. "Yes, dear! Got it! No gambling!"

Eunice realized she was going to have to keep an eye on him.

On the casino floor, Tinkles was chasing a half cat and half fish creature swimming under the glass beneath his paws. Drac walked by, so Dennis and Winnie did their best to block his view of the huge dog.

Drac was so focused on his goal that he didn't even notice. He spotted Murray, Frank, and Griffin and beelined straight to them.

"Have you guys seen Mavis? I have to find her," he said.

"Why, buddy? What's going on?" Griffin wondered.

"I'm going to tell her about Ericka," Dracula told them. "I can't lie to my own daughter anymore. She's the most important person in the world to me. I have to tell her the truth." As he said it, Drac noticed Ericka walking toward the back of the casino, looking around.

He started to follow her, saying, "Right after I talk to Ericka."

Outside the casino, Johnny was taking in the sights when Mavis came rushing up.

"Johnny, have you seen my dad?" she asked. She wanted to find him so they could all be together, just like she had planned.

"Maybe he's with Bob." Johnny shrugged.

"Why would he be with Bob?" Mavis said, thinking that Johnny could be confusing at times.

"Bob's a great guy!" Johnny explained, as if she should have known.

Just over Johnny's shoulder, Mavis spotted her dad moving quickly through the main casino.

"There he is," she said, immediately noticing that Dracula was following Ericka.

"Who? Bob?" Johnny asked.

Mavis rushed off without answering.

At the rear of the casino, Ericka glanced over her shoulder to make sure that no one was following. Then she ducked behind a curtain. Drac hid for a second so she wouldn't see him, then followed Ericka. He had no idea that Mavis was behind him, joining in the chase.

CHAPTER TEN

Ericka stopped at a giant carving of a face in the side of a long wall. The eyes were hidden handles that she used to open a door leading to a passageway. She went inside. Drac followed, nearly dropping down a deep hole, but he caught himself in time.

Ericka hurried ahead down a narrow crawl space. She had to scale the rocks by hand, but Drac followed easily, floating over the hazards.

Behind them, Mavis approached the face carving. She tried to push the eyes, nose, forehead . . . but nothing happened. Finally she gave up and turned into a bat so she could be small enough to crawl through the opening in the mouth.

Ericka and Drac reached a pool with a giant statue of a head in the middle. Not realizing Drac was there, she began to take her captain clothes off.

Dracula covered his eyes. When he opened them, Ericka was now wearing a wet suit that she'd had on underneath her clothing.

She popped a breathing device into her mouth and dove into the water, straight through the nostril of the giant sculpture.

With a splash, Drac dove into the water and swam after her.

Mavis heard the splash and flew quickly in that direction, following the sounds.

Ericka emerged from the water into the ruins of a once-magnificent underwater palace. Across the long chamber was another kind of device held up by a giant stone hand. It glowed, pulsing with power. It was obviously magical.

"There it is," she said excitedly to herself. "The device."

Drac came out of the water behind her, awed and confused by what he saw.

He watched as Ericka began to move eagerly forward toward the device, but she accidentally stepped on a stone and set off a booby trap. An axe flew out of the wall, straight toward her.

Dracula grabbed the axe in midair, tossing it aside as if it was nothing.

"You saved my life." Ericka was genuinely surprised to find out that Drac had not only followed her, but stepped in to rescue her as well.

"Of course. Why wouldn't I?" Drac said, moving them out of harm's way.

"I just can't believe you would do that for a human." Ericka tried to process what had happened.

"Humans, monsters, what's the difference?" Dracula asked her. "Humans are people too."

"Uh, yeah . . . right. What are you doing here?" She felt like everything she'd been taught about monsters was slowly being brought into question by Drac's kindness.

Drac tried to cover for the fact that he'd been following her. "Oh, uh . . . Vampires can predict the future," he lied, "so I knew you would need help."

Ericka tilted her head. "Never heard that before."

"Oh yeah, it's a well known fact. Uh . . . what are *you* doing here, anyway?" He changed the subject.

"Oh, well, I'm here to get that." Ericka had to come up with an excuse . . . fast. She pointed at the device. "It's a . . . family heirloom. Yeah. It was lost . . . at sea, and uh, my grandfather is—was—totally obsessed with getting it back."

Flustered, Ericka tried to change the subject and get rid of Dracula.

"Well, any-hoo, thanks for saving my life, but I can take it from here." She didn't need his help. That was, until she took a step back—and a second flying axe swung at her.

Again, Drac caught it and threw it to the side.

"Whew. Gotta be a little more careful. How many times can you save my life, right?" She chuckled nervously.

"I don't know. Every time?" he suggested.

"Really?" Ericka considered this development. "Prove it!"

Feeling confident that Dracula would save her,

Ericka skipped toward the stone, setting off every booby trap.

Drac saved her from arrows. From darts. From snakes. From axes . . .

She reached the device and turned around, gushing with adrenaline. "That was incredible!"

Then she saw that Drac was riddled with the booby trap objects. He looked like a giant pincushion!

When she didn't immediately grab the device, he asked, "Don't you want to get your family heirloom thingie?"

"Oh. Right." Ericka turned back and took the device from the giant fingers. Suddenly the room began to shake. The fingers curled into a fist and shot up toward the ceiling.

"Uh-oh." Drac gasped.

The fist hit the ceiling, and part of the roof came tumbling down. The whole room began to collapse.

"Run!" Drac shouted, and they both took off, back the way they had come.

Despite her head start, Drac could see that Ericka was not going to make it out in time. He turned on the superspeed and swept her up, just before she was going to be crushed by falling debris.

As the room collapsed around them, Drac and Ericka zipped to safety. They shot out of the nose of the statue and landed on a large piece of rubble. It was so close. Relieved, they awkwardly chuckled and gave each other a tender look.

"Here, let me get that." Ericka grabbed an axe that was stuck in Drac, just as Mavis found them together.

"Dad?" The first thing she saw was that her dad was still a pincushion.

"Mavis?" Drac asked.

"What are you doing to my father?" Mavis shrieked at Ericka. Her eyes blazed red as she levitated Ericka up into the air and left her dangling.

"Wait! AHHH!" Ericka screamed.

"Mavis! Stop! Put her down!" Drac told her.

Mavis refused. "No, she's trying to hurt you! Why can't you see that?"

Drac leaned into her and whispered softly, "I zinged."

Mavis was so stunned, she dropped Ericka. "What?"

"Because I . . . because I . . . zinged. With Ericka." He nodded toward the crumpled captain.

"No, that can't be true. You only zing once," Mavis insisted.

"That's what I thought too." Drac shrugged.

"Zing? What's a zing?" Ericka stood and dusted herself off.

"Uh, well, it's a thing for monsters," Drac explained. "It's kind of like our love at first sight."

This was way too much for Ericka. She began to feel conflicted, even guilty.

"What? No, no, you don't even know me," she protested.

"Well, not yet, but we're just—"

Ericka interrupted. "What? No, no, you don't understand. I can't be with you. I could never be with someone like you. I could never be with a monster." She turned and walked away, carrying the device.

Drac was heartbroken. Mavis went up to him.

"Dad, I'm so sorry." Mavis wrapped her arms around her dad.

Drac sighed. "It doesn't matter. You heard what she said."

"Maybe it's for the best," Mavis told him. "There's something not right about her."

"Yeah, you're probably right." Drac walked away from Mavis, leaving her alone.

"But a zing never lies," Mavis muttered to herself.

CHAPTER ELEVEN

The monsters boarded the ship after their night in Atlantis.

"Check it out," Murray said. He showed off his wrapping, which he had had tattooed with a Chinese symbol. "Got it last night. It means 'journey of the spirit'!"

The Nine-Tailed Fox passed by and said, "Actually, it means, 'idiot butt.'"

Murray stared at the tattoo. "Wh-what?"

Griffin and his girlfriend, Crystal, walked in. She had a huge floating ring on her finger.

"Oh, honey, I can't believe we got married last night!"

the Invisible Girlfriend cooed, showing off the ring to everyone.

"Wait, come again?" Griffin was surprised. He must have forgotten! He looked down at the floating ring and stammered, "Ah! Oh yeah, oh, we, we did because . . . ?" Tiny drops of water formed midair and started to pool on the floor, right where Griffin was standing.

"Griffin, I can see you sweating," she accused.

"What?" Griffin tried to wipe it off. "No, I'm not! Honey, that's, uh, condensation."

As he tried to explain himself, Frank and Eunice were walking back. Frank had no arms!

"I told you not to gamble, and what happened?" Eunice screeched.

"I lost an arm, and another arm," Frank sighed.

Eunice was so mad. "Right, Frank. Now look at you. Where are you going to get another set of arms?"

"I don't know," Frank admitted, "but I'll figure it out, okay?"

"Figure out how you're gonna go to the bathroom, Frank!" Eunice yelled.

In the laundry room, Murray tried to scrub his tattoo off, but it didn't even fade. He sighed and climbed inside the washing machine.

Drac walked into his cabin, miserable. He took off his cape, then realized there was something in his neck. He plucked out a stone needle from the Atlantis booby trap. It reminded him of his time with Ericka. Drac let out a long, sad sigh.

Down below, in Van Helsing's room, Ericka was showing her great-grandfather the device. She was sad, but of course Van Helsing didn't notice.

"You got it," he said, grabbing it from her hands. "Finally, the end of monsters is upon us. Tomorrow night we unleash the power of the device—" There was a playful glint in the old man's eyes. All his dreams were about to come true.

Ericka was conflicted. "He saved my life."

"Uh, what?" Van Helsing asked.

"He saved my life." Ericka pinched her lips together thoughtfully. "And then he and his daughter, the way they talk, the way they argue . . ." She considered what she'd seen. "How they worry about each other—they were so . . . human." It was confusing, and Ericka was still trying to make sense of all this new information.

Van Helsing saw her hesitation. "No!" he exclaimed. "They have no feelings, no consciousness. They are monsters. We are Van Helsings. And the time has come to fulfill our legacy."

Ericka shrunk away from him as the device glowed with anger.

For the cruise ship passengers, nothing seemed out of the ordinary.

Eunice was nearly ready for the party too. She put on her dress and then, forgetting what had happened, asked Frank to zip up her dress. She turned to see Frank . . . with lobster claws that he had attached to his body in place of his missing arms!

"Where did you get those?" Eunice asked, startled.

"Oh, uh . . . from the seafood buffet," Frank said. For fun, he made clickity-clackety sounds with them. "Hehe," Frank laughed. "I kinda like them."

102

When the monsters arrived at the party, they walked through the doors to the room . . . and somehow ended up on a balcony overlooking the ocean at the back side of the island of Atlantis.

"I thought they said the party was this way?" Eunice said, wondering where they'd made a wrong turn.

All the monsters had gone to the same place. It was clear that the party wasn't ready yet, and they began to grumble, confused about where they were supposed to go.

Suddenly they heard a deep, muffled beat coming from underwater, and lights started to flicker. A huge dance floor rose from the ocean, complete with a DJ playing party music from a clamshell DJ booth! Then a bridge rose up that connected the balcony and the dance floor, and the monsters rushed over it and started to dance. Next, the Kraken emerged from the water and began to sing.

Drac stood in the center of the dance floor, as happy monsters moved and grooved to the music around him. He didn't know that Mavis was watching him, unsure what to do about the news that he had zinged with someone other than her mother. She barely paid attention to Johnny and Dennis, who were dancing next to her.

"I can't believe my dad zinged with someone who's trying to kill him," Mavis said.

"The zing makes you do crazy things," Johnny said as he boogied.

"Really, Johnny?" Mavis shook her head.

Johnny nudged her to accept her dad. "Love is an infinite enigma that is beyond our understanding," Johnny explained calmly while break-dancing to the music. "You and I were two halves a world apart. But then we followed the strands of destiny and were brought together, and our halves made one whole."

Mavis asked, "But what if she and he—"

Johnny told her, "You must release all the negativity and look within. Your bond is unbreakable."

Mavis looked at Drac, then back at Johnny.

"You're right, honey. Wow, thanks!" Mavis gave him a quick kiss, then hurried off to talk to Drac.

Dennis was impressed. "Whoa, you sounded pretty smart, Dad."

104

Johnny smiled. "Oh, *that*? It was the philosophy of Sifu Sing from my favorite TV show when I was a kid, *Kung Fu Shaolin Monk Master*."

"Cool!" Dennis said. He was even more impressed now!

Mavis walked up to Drac. "Dad, you have to talk to Ericka."

"Cool," Drac said flatly. He wasn't really listening. Then he registered what she had said, and asked, "What?"

"I know what I said before, but maybe I overreacted a teeeeeensy bit. It's just, the thought of losing you . . ."

"What? What are you talking about, losing me?" Drac asked.

Mavis blurted out what she had been thinking ever since she'd learned about her dad and Ericka. "Well, obviously, after you get married, you're gonna live on the ship and travel the world—"

Dracula butted in. "Whoa, whoa, slow down! Mavis, there are two things I can promise you. One: Nothing

105

can ever take me from you and all my family. Two: I will never live on a boat."

Mavis burst into a relieved smile. "Dad!"

He gave her a big hug. "You're my cute little tarantula," Drac told her, holding her tight. "How can I ever leave you?"

Mavis smiled, then turned serious again. "Now, seriously, go talk to her." Mavis said.

"I can't," Drac replied, stepping back. "You heard what she said. She could never be with someone like me."

"No, Dad. You're just a half, and you have to follow your destiny to find an infinite whole," Mavis said. It had sounded so good when Johnny had said it, but Drac just looked confused.

"You sound like Johnny," he said.

"The point is, you can't deny a zing," Mavis told him, now trying to explain it in her own way. "So go to her. Now!"

Drac was blown away at how amazing his daughter had turned out. "Okay, I'm on it," Drac said, and then hurried away to find Ericka.

CHAPTER TWELVE

Suddenly the lights went out and the music stopped. The crowd on the dance floor looked around, confused.

From the DJ booth, the DJ began to raise his voice. "Hey, man, you're not allowed up here," he said. Then there was a scream and a thud.

When the lights came back on, Van Helsing's face was projected on large screens. The monsters shuddered in fear.

"Who is this?" Drac asked.

Over the loudspeaker and displays, Van Helsing responded directly to Drac.

"I know you recognize me: your greatest rival!" Van

Helsing said. "It is I, Abraham Van Helsing!"

"After all these years?" Drac joked. "You look . . . awful."

Van Helsing ignored him. "To fulfill my family's—" he continued, but Drac interrupted him.

"I'm sorry. I can't even hear what you're saying. I'm just so focused on how gross you are!" Drac said.

Van Helsing didn't stop. "Always with the quick insults. . . . Well, this will shut you up, and all monsters!" he said, taking out the device.

Drac recognized it. "Uh, that's just Ericka's family heirloom thingie."

"You fool!" Van Helsing crowed. "Not only is Ericka the ship's captain, but she also happens to be . . ."

"I'm his great-granddaughter," Ericka said, appearing from her hiding place. "I'm Ericka Van Helsing."

Dracula and Mavis gasped.

"I knew there was something wrong with her!" Mavis whispered.

Van Helsing went on. "Now that we're all caught up, let's get back to the dying. With this device, my family legacy will finally be fulfilled." He opened the device, which was a canister, and took out a scroll. He laid it on the piano. It was sheet music. He cracked his fingers.

"Terrifying!" Griffin yelled.

Van Helsing began to play the music. "Listen. It's the melody of your destruction."

The music traveled underwater to where the Kraken was going about his chores, ironing. He heard the beat and was hypnotized. His eyes turned green, and he turned into an evil creature. He rose up behind Van Helsing as Drac and the others looked on in fear.

"Everybody out, now!" Drac yelled.

The Kraken attacked, swatting at guests with his tentacles.

The monsters scattered and ran for their lives . . . but the Kraken used another tentacle to destroy the bridge back to the ship. Monsters that could fly tried to get away by air, but the Kraken swatted them down.

Drac growled. He had to stop the madman, once and for all. He flew toward Van Helsing. In his anger, he didn't see the Kraken.

"Drac, no!" Johnny warned him, but the Kraken grabbed Drac in midair.

"Ahhh!" yelled Drac, in pain, as the Kraken squeezed him tightly with a giant tentacle.

Drac struggled to break free, fly away, change shape—anything—but the Kraken's hold on him was too strong. Drac was getting weaker by the second. He used what he thought might be his last breaths to call out Van Helsing on his evil scheme. "The cruise . . . all this . . . it was a trap . . . ," he said in small bursts of breath.

"Yes, and you all fell for it! What monster can refuse a discounted vacation?" Van Helsing said, pleased with his plan.

Ericka looked at Drac. "I'm sorry," she said, and it seemed genuine.

Drac was devastated. He stopped fighting and slumped over, giving up. For the first time in his long life, he looked mortal.

Van Helsing gloated. "Time for the 'immortal' Dracula to die."

"Dad!" Mavis yelled. She tried to attack Van Helsing and Ericka to save her father, but the Kraken held her down.

Then the Kraken turned his attention back to Drac and tossed him into his mouth . . . or tried to. Drac began to fall . . .

"No!" Ericka yelled. She hurled herself toward Drac and the Kraken, bouncing off Blobby and launching herself into the air to catch Drac. She saved his life!

No one was more surprised than Van Helsing. "Ericka?" he asked.

Ericka and Drac fell together, sliding off the dance floor and into the water, but Ericka grabbed the edge of the dance floor just in time. She held on tight as she struggled to keep Drac's head above water, since he was still very weak.

The Kraken realized they weren't a threat anymore and went back to wreaking havoc. Van Helsing cackled with delight.

"You can't do this," Ericka told her great-grandfather. "You're wrong about monsters."

"What?" Van Helsing replied, even though he had heard every word.

She turned away from him, and toward Drac. "I'm so sorry, Drac. I was trying to kill you this whole time, but I'm glad I tried, because I got to know you, and I saw what a wonderful ... *person* ... you are, and now I realize how wrong I was. How wrong all of this is."

Drac didn't reply. His eyes were closed, and it wasn't clear if he could even hear her or if he was already too far gone.

Ericka turned back to Van Helsing. "They're not animals! They have families, they care about each other. They laugh, just like we do. They argue, just like we do. They love, just like we do."

"Lies!" Van Helsing hollered.

"I know because I *zinged*," Ericka insisted.

At that, Drac's eyes popped open.

"What's a zing?" Van Helsing asked.

"It's a monster thing," Ericka said, then added a dig. "You wouldn't understand."

"It's like true love!" Drac said, smiling and looking much more alive.

Van Helsing was horrified. "Love!" he scoffed, as if love didn't matter to him at all.

Before Drac or Ericka could say more, the Kraken tried to attack them again. This time, Drac was full of energy after learning that Ericka had zinged with him, too. He fought back against the Kraken!

"Well, I guess the legacy ends with me," said Van Helsing.

"It's time to start a new legacy," Ericka added.

"A monster-human legacy," Drac pitched in.

"Nooo!" Van Helsing yelled.

Drac tried to attack the Kraken.

"Drac, no, wait!" Johnny cried out.

Drac was going to attack again when Johnny shouted, "Wait! No!" and "Drac, stop!"

"What? What is it?" Drac asked impatiently. He didn't have time to waste.

"Van Helsing's beats are controlling the giant octopus thingie," Johnny blurted out, having just realized it himself. "If there's one thing I hate, it's an evil DJ."

"That's why I'm trying to smash him!" Drac said.

"No can do!" Johnny insisted. "Fighting bad vibes with bad vibes just makes super-harsh vibes!"

Dracula looked confused. "What are you talking about, Johnny?"

"We need positive energy!" Johnny said. At that,

Johnny walked to a spot across the dance floor from where Van Helsing was stationed in the DJ booth and began unpacking his backpack, which contained a laptop, speakers, and headphones. "Get ready for a DJ battle!" Johnny said proudly.

"You just carry all that stuff around with you?" Drac asked, amazed.

"Once a bar mitzvah DJ, always a bar mitzvah DJ," Johnny said, as if it was completely normal to carry all of that with him just in case he needed to deejay. "We're going to use good music to defeat his evil music!" Johnny explained.

Drac finally understood, but he wasn't convinced Johnny's plan would work.

"But your music isn't good. It's terrible!" Drac complained.

Johnny didn't seem to care what Drac thought of his music. "Drac, trust me! I know the tunes, but you've got the power!" Johnny said while scrolling through his music files. He knew the opening song needed to be just right.

A few seconds later, the Kraken was about to move

in for yet another attack, when Johnny found the perfect song to play. "Ooh! Got it! Play this!" Johnny told Drac.

Drac zapped Johnny's computer to power the music, and the classic song "Good Vibrations," by the Beach Boys, began to blast from the speakers.

The Kraken seemed to like it! He swayed to the sunny beat, and his eyes began to change back to normal.

"Wait, what is that noise?" Van Helsing looked around to discover that Drac and Johnny were playing the music. To counter it, Van Helsing waved his hand over the device to make its evil beat stronger. Soon the evil beat overpowered "Good Vibrations," and the Kraken went back to attack mode.

In seconds, the Kraken was towering over Sunny.

"I'm too young to die!" Sunny shouted.

Just then, Ericka stepped in and saved Sunny!

"Yay! I'm alive!" Sunny squealed.

"Whoa, Van Helsing's music is too powerful!" Johnny said, considering the problem. "We're gonna need something even more positive." After a quick search, he found another song. "Now, Drac!"

Drac saw that Johnny had chosen "Don't Worry, Be Happy" by Bobby McFerrin, and he zapped the computer again to play the song.

The Kraken smiled.

"Really?" Drac asked Johnny, surprised by the choice in music.

"It has a nice message!" Johnny assured him, but since the Kraken started to get angry again, it was clear Johnny needed to choose another song.

Van Helsing wasn't amused. "No more games. This ends now!" he said.

CHAPTER THIRTEEN

Drac knew what they needed to do. "Johnny, we need the most brain-dominating, toe-tappinating song in the history of all the universe!" Drac said.

Johnny panicked as he searched through his music list. "I don't know! There's too many choices!" he said. Then his eyes lit up. "No, wait. This, this is it."

The Kraken's giant jaws opened up over Johnny and Drac, as he prepared to attack again.

Suddenly the sound of five unforgettable opening beats pulsed out of the speakers. It was the beginning of "The Macarena"!

The Kraken's eyes went back to normal, and he

opened his mouth and stuck out his tongue. Soon Johnny started dancing, and then the rest of the monsters joined him and the Kraken on the dance floor!

Van Helsing was furious! "Stop it! Stop that dancing!" he said, but his fingers started tapping the beat against his will. Soon his right hand shot up to touch his left shoulder in one of the classic moves of the Macarena dance. "Stop that!" he told it, and tried to pull it down with his left hand . . . but instead his left hand crossed over the first to touch his right shoulder in the next move of the dance.

The Macarena was defeating the evil beat from Van Helsing's device!

"Hey, Johnny's corny music is defeating the evil music," Vlad said. "I kinda like it." He started doing the Macarena too.

Van Helsing scowled as the evil sheet music began to disappear. "No!" he yelled. Then, against his will, he started dancing the Macarena again. "Ahh! I'm a slave to the rhythm!" Van Helsing shouted, unable to stop moving to the catchy song. As he did the next move in the dance, he fell off the DJ booth and then rolled onto the dance floor . . . and then rolled right off it again as he and his chair went over the edge, high above the water.

Ericka gasped as she watched what seemed to be her great-grandfather's last moments.

Drac realized he had to do something, so at the last minute he turned into a bat and flew after Van Helsing.

"Drac, what are you doing?" Frank called out.

"You gotta be greater than the haters," Murray explained to Frank, and then watched with admiration as Drac rescued Van Helsing right before he would have hit the water and, most likely, drawn his last breath.

Without a word, Drac then flew back to the dance party carrying Van Helsing, and transformed back into human form as he set his nemesis down.

Van Helsing looked up at Drac with a mix of awe and confusion. For some reason, though, he sounded very angry even though he was actually grateful. "Why? Why after everything would you save my life?"

"Because, basically," Drac replied, "we are all the same. Claws or hands. Two eyes, three eyes—"

Harry Three-Eye stepped in front of Drac and waved at Van Helsing to illustrate Drac's point.

Then other monsters spoke up.

"Green skin!" a witch added.

"No skin!" said a skeleton.

A fish man shouted, "Gills!"

A monster with a furry face said, "Furry face!"

Carl said, "Prickly."

"Scary handsome!" Vlad said, smiling and showing off.

"Frightened?" Van Helsing asked.

"Yep," Drac said. "We are all one," he told Van Helsing. The monsters had proved his point.

Ericka was convinced too. She turned to Drac and said, "You are amazing."

Drac and Ericka looked at one another, and suddenly they both zinged!

Tinkles jumped on Drac, practically smothering him with doggie kisses.

"Wait, what? Bob?" Drac asked, wondering why Bob would be licking his face like a dog. Then he realized that Bob was the dog Tinkles in disguise! "Tinkles?" he asked.

Mavis hadn't had a clue. "Bob was Tinkles in disguise?" she asked.

Dennis and Winnie just giggled.

While the family had a happy reunion, Van Helsing was alone with the rest of the monsters on the dance floor. "Heh, I feel kind of silly now. For decades I have hunted your kind, persecuted you."

All the monsters murmured in agreement.

"The only thing I can do to make it up to you is . . . give you a thirty percent refund," Van Helsing went on. He thought he'd get a big cheer, but no one was excited about that, and La Llorona wept, although that wasn't out of the ordinary.

"Oh, all right, a full refund!" Van Helsing gave in.

This time, all the monsters cheered.

EPILOGUE

Drac and Ericka lounged on the cruise ship's deck, holding hands as the family had fun in the pool. Even Van Helsing was having a good time!

Suddenly a wave of wolf pups stampeded through the pool area, followed by the fish man.

"Can someone get the parents?" the fish man begged.

The parents? Drac and the others suddenly realized they hadn't seen Wayne and Wanda since soon after they'd boarded the cruise ship.

"Where's Wayne and Wanda?" Drac asked.

"Oops." Ericka grimaced. She knew exactly where the parents had gone off to, and led the way to the closet where she and Van Helsing had hidden them.

Wayne and Wanda were just where they had been left, frozen in place. Drac was preparing to save them when he noticed Wayne staring at him and trying to talk.

"Mmmmmmm . . . mmmmm . . . mmmm!" Wayne mumbled, struggling to move.

"Don't worry. I got you!" Drac said calmly.

Then Drac zapped them and they were magically unfrozen! Drac didn't get the thank-you he'd been expecting.

"Why did you do that?" Wayne protested as soon as he could talk.

"Huh?" Drac looked sideways at his friend.

Wayne sighed. "This was the most relaxing vacation we've ever had!"

Wanda agreed. "We're gonna book it again for the holidays."

A few days later, back at the Hotel Transylvania, everything was busy as usual. Guests were checking in, zombies were handling the luggage, and Mavis was working in the lobby.

"Checking in?" Mavis asked a fish man who had booked a hotel room after meeting the family on the cruise.

"Yes, thank you," said the fish man.

"Great! I have a room all ready for you," Mavis said.

She didn't notice as Drac and Ericka snuck into an elevator and went to the thirteenth floor.

Drac peeked into the hallway, and Ericka sneaked close behind him. They went to the attic, and then to the hotel's rooftop.

"What's going on, sneaky pants?" Ericka asked Drac.

"Oh, nothing," Drac said nervously. "I just wanted to make sure no one would bother us."

"Why? Are you going to suck my blood, blah, blah, blah?" she joked.

It took all of Drac's strength to not correct her by saying that he doesn't say "blah, blah, blah," but he stayed calm. He got down on one knee and held out a box. "No, I was going to ask if you would marry me," he said kindly, opening the box to reveal a beautiful spider-shaped ring with a red jewel at the center.

It was actually a real spider, and it crawled to Ericka's ring finger.

"Well, what do you say?" Drac asked Ericka.

"I . . . woo ba-doo-bi-dee?" Ericka said. Drac began to sweat. Ericka tried again, saying, "I mean, I woo be doo bee dee?"

At that, everyone came to the roof: Mavis, Johnny, and Dennis, Wayne and Wanda, and the whole gang.

"What did she say?" they asked.

"I'm not sure," Drac admitted.

Ericka pulled herself together. "Yes!" she said happily.

"Woo-hoo!" Drac yelled, and everyone cheered.

As Tinkles tackled the bride-and-groom-to-be, it was the beginning of another beautiful chapter for Drac, Mavis, and Hotel Transylvania.

ABOUT THE AUTHOR

Stacia Deutsch is the author of more than fifty children's books, including the eight-book, award-winning chapter book series Blast to the Past. She has also written the tween novel *Mean Ghouls* as well as books for the Nancy Drew and the Clue Crew and The Boxcar Children series. Stacia has been on the *New York Times* bestseller list for the novelizations of the *Cloudy with a Chance of Meatballs* and *The Smurfs* movies. For new releases and school visit information, visit StaciaDeutsch.com.